PUFF

PROFESSOR E
CRUNCHY

Professor Branestawm deci... ... can invent something better than Magic Foam washing-up liquid. Something so superior it will do away with washing-up altogether. The Professor seems to have been amazingly successful this time and it looks like being one of his best inventions ever. So he decides to throw a party – a party where people will simply eat their plates and glasses – a party involving no washing-up!

In *Professor Branestawm's Hair-Raising Idea*, the Professor gets it into his head to invent a machine capable of giving Mrs Flittersnoop a new hair-style every day. But Mr Percy Pompadour is furious, he knows no one will pay a fortune to come to his hair-dressing salon anymore; so the Professor agrees to lend it to him. Mrs Trumpington Smaul is his first customer, and that's when things start getting a little out of control.

These two stories were specially written for Professor Branestawm's younger fans. They are published together for the first time and will leave all his fans begging for more.

By the same author

PROFESSOR BRANESTAWM'S MOUSE WAR
PROFESSOR BRANESTAWM'S POCKET MOTOR CAR

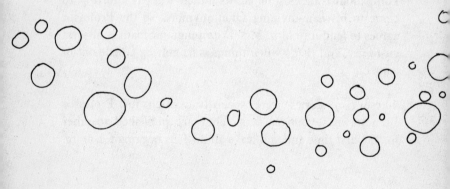

NORMAN HUNTER

Professor Branestawm's Crunchy Crockery

Illustrated by Gerald Rose

PUFFIN BOOKS

Professor Branestawm's Crunchy Crockery dedicated to
Penny with love

Professor Branestawm's Hair-Raising Idea dedicated to
Joanna Lumley and James with great affection

Professor Branestawm would like to thank Sally Cobb for
telling him the special hairdressing words in this story.

PUFFIN BOOKS

Published by the Penguin Group
Penguin Books Ltd, 27 Wrights Lane, London w8 5tz, England
Penguin Books USA Inc., 375 Hudson Street, New York, New York 10014, USA
Penguin Books Australia Ltd, Ringwood, Victoria, Australia
Penguin Books Canada Ltd, 10 Alcorn Avenue, Toronto, Ontario, Canada m4v 3b2
Penguin Books (NZ) Ltd, 182–190 Wairau Road, Auckland 10, New Zealand

Penguin Books Ltd, Registered Offices: Harmondsworth, Middlesex, England

Professor Branestawm's Crunchy Crockery first published by The Bodley Head 1983
Professor Branestawm's Hair-Raising Idea first published by The Bodley Head 1983
Published together in Puffin Books 1993
1 3 5 7 9 10 8 6 4 2

Text copyright © Norman Hunter, 1983
Illustrations copyright © Gerald Rose, 1983
All rights reserved

The moral right of the author has been asserted

Printed in England by Clays Ltd, St Ives plc
Filmset in Monophoto Ehrhardt

CONTENTS

Professor Branestawm's
Crunchy Crockery

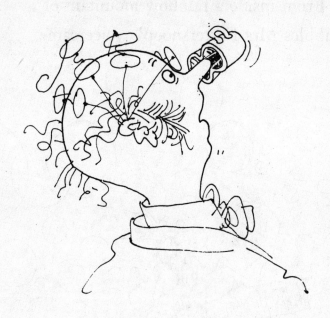

"Really, um, ah, Mrs Flittersnoop," said
Professor Branestawm, "I hardly think you
should have a bubble bath in the kitchen."
From inside a rainbow mountain of
bubbles Mrs Flittersnoop's voice came

out like the steam from a hearty kettle.

"No indeed, I'm sure, sir," she said. "I'm not having a bubble bath. I'm washing up the tea things with this new softer than soft, kind to the hands, delicately perfumed Magic Foam."

"It must be very difficult to find the dishes," said the Professor, fighting his way through bouncing bubbles that burst on his five pairs of spectacles.

"Yes indeed," said Mrs Flittersnoop, washing the Professor's face by mistake for a pudding plate. "And of course one has to rinse them in plain water afterwards or they taste funny."

The Professor licked the magic
bubbles off his face and thought they
tasted very funny indeed. "I shall invent
a way of doing away with washing-up,"
he said firmly.

"But how will you do it?" Mrs
Flittersnoop asked.

"Very simple," said the Professor. "Edible china and glass. Crunchy crockery, palatable pie dishes and tasty teacups. You could use that edible paper you find on the bottom of macaroons for plates, and edible jelly could be turned into glasses. With a few simple chemical variations, we shall have edible crockery and cutlery and nothing to wash up at all!"

He shot off into his inventory, leaving
Mrs Flittersnoop sitting on the pedal bin
trying hard to imagine cutting someone
a nice slice of edible teapot but not
succeeding much.

The inventing noises from the
Professor's inventory were a bit different
from the usually unusual. There were
no bangs, very few crashes and no
explosions worth mentioning. There was
a slight smell of elderly smoked haddock
tinged with cough mixture and helped
along with a whiff or five of railway

tunnels, but otherwise everything was so extraordinarily ordinary that Mrs Flittersnoop began to wonder if she should go to her sister Aggie's in Lower Pagwell for a few days, just in case anything blew up unexpectedly.

But she didn't and it didn't, and at last Professor Branestawm came out of his inventory, carrying in each hand a tray of very crocky-looking crockery, some slightly ghastly glasses and a few gnarled knives and funny forks.

"Have an, er, um, teacup," he said,
holding out a blue and pink thing that
looked like an unlikely twisted yoghurt
carton.

"Very nice, I'm sure, sir," said Mrs
Flittersnoop, not meaning it, but wanting
to be polite. "What shall I do with it?"

"Eat it," said the Professor, crunching
up a plate with crinkly edges.

Mrs Flittersnoop took a cautious bite. *Crunch, crunch, um, ah, yum.* It tasted very good. "A little on the sweet side perhaps, sir," she said, "but very nice!"

"Er, um, crunch, yes, munch, munch," replied the Professor with his hands full of five pairs of spectacles and his mouth full of crinkly plate. "You see what this means? No more washing-up! You eat the china and other things, as well as the, um, ah, food. We must have a party to demonstrate it!"

Professor Branestawm had put
up a marquee in his garden and
his crunchy crockery party was
raging very happily.

Mrs Flittersnoop had cooked extremely edible food to go on the edible plates and be eaten with the edible knives and forks.

Colonel Dedshott, the Professor's best friend, said, "By Jove, Branestawm, y'know, this will be a great thing for Army. Leave washing-up squads free to

fight enemy. Clean up the foe instead of the dishes, my word, what!" He crunched up a trifle of his trifle plate and blew out his whiskers to show he approved.

The Mayor of Pagwell was finding a mouthful or two of dinner-plate went very well with steak and kidney pudding.

The Mayoress of Pagwell, with her little finger sticking out at just the right angle, raised a cup of coffee to her lips, but she kept up the politeness for too long. The edible cup dissolved and the coffee sploshed all over her new dress.

Actually, this made it look much better
as the coffee quietened down the rather
shriekish design.

"Well," said the Professor, "I, um,
ah, think my invention has proved itself
to be an unusual success."

Oh goodness, he shouldn't have said
that. The Mayoress, having lost her cup
of coffee, poured some more into a saucer
and drank out of that. Not a very Mayoress
kind of thing to do in company. And
Professor Branestawm's inventions were
always rather sticklers for good manners.
The saucer wobbled a bit and the
Mayoress spilt coffee down her dress again,
which made it look almost attractive.

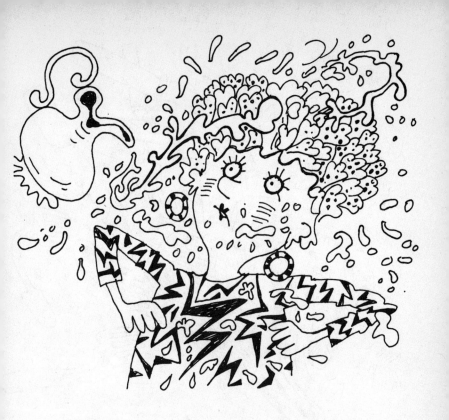

The coffee jug then sprang up and poured coffee all over her head.

"Ow!" cried the Mayoress.

"Oh, I, um, er," said the Professor, not knowing what else to say. But he was saved from saying anything by a teacup that pinched his nose.

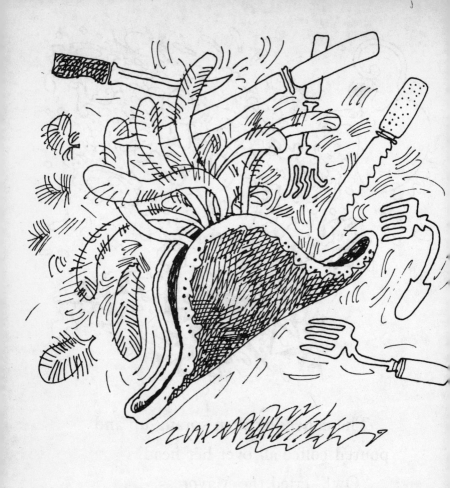

The trifle dish slid out and
began chasing the Mayoress round and
round the tent.

Then the edible crockery and cutlery
really took over. Knives and forks
chopped up Colonel Dedshott's hat and
fed it to the trifle, which wouldn't eat it.

Two milk jugs attacked a sausage from opposite ends and started a very impolite fight when they met in the middle.

Colonel Dedshott drew his sword to ward off a flank attack by six non-matching saucers.

The tent was worse than ten assorted battlefields as edible crockery and cutlery attacked the people who had been attacking food. Gravy mixed with shrieks flew about.

Then a bowl of strawberries emptied itself on to Mrs Trumpington Smawl's hat. This was followed by an attack from a jug that was very generous with a helping of best cream.

Mrs Trumpington Smawl let out a shriek . . .

EEEEEEEEK!

... so loud that Colonel Dedshott's horse, which was tied up outside to a tent peg, reared up and kicked out in all directions.

The ropes became entangled with the horse's legs and the marquee was pulled down.

In the confusion which followed
Colonel Dedshott blew his bugle.

41

Thank goodness the Catapult
Cavaliers heard his call for help. They
appeared from nowhere and pulled the
guests from under the collapsed tent.

The battle of the tent had ended with edible crockery trampled underfoot and not very edible leftover food left all over the place.

But the Catapult Cavaliers soon ate up all that, because soldiers are always hungry through having to left-right, left-right, shun and slope arms day and night.

"Oh dear me, I'm sure, sir!" said Mrs Flittersnoop, surveying the mess after everyone had gone home. "Your edible crockery certainly saved the washing-up, sir, but this mess is going to take some clearing up and no mistake.

And begging your pardon, sir, if I might make so bold, in future I'd rather wash up the crockery and cutlery with biological washing-up liquid that makes everything ten times cleaner than clean with ten pence off the next purchase."

So that was the end of Professor Branestawm's marvellous edible china, glass and cutlery, except that the Mayor did have a few slight pains in his corporation afterwards.

Professor Branestawm's Hair-Raising Idea

Professor Branestawm sat in a fancy
chair in Mr Percy Pompadour's even
fancier hairdressing salon. He was
looking at a row of ladies sitting under
what looked like space helmets, and, just
as he was wondering when they would

take off into outer space, one of them
took off her helmet. It was Mrs
Flittersnoop, his housekeeper, who had
saved up to come to Mr Pompadour's
for a highly special hair-do.

As she came towards the Professor, Mrs Flittersnoop suddenly let out a supersonic screech, waved her hands in the air and cried, "Oh, oh, oh, how awful!"

"It is only, um, er, me," said the Professor. "I expect you didn't recognize me with your new hair-style."

"Oh no, indeed, sir," gasped Mrs

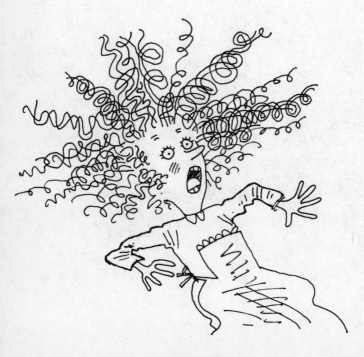

Flittersnoop. "I recognized *you*, but I've just seen myself in the mirror over there and I hardly recognize myself. This awful hair-style! I look like one of those cakes with coconut bits sticking out. And I paid so much for it, I shall never be able to afford another!"

"Tut, er, tut," said the Professor. "You must calm down!" he cried excitedly. "I shall invent a wonderful machine that will give you any kind of hair-style you like." And he rushed home to do it.

Professor Branestawm, his head full of astonishing ideas and his hands full of twiddly tools, soon got inventing in his inventory.

"I shall invent a machine that styles women's hair without all this bother," he said to himself. "No need for them to be fastened up with little coloured cylinders with holes in them and sit cooking in space helmets. I am going to change all that."

Changing all that also changed the Professor's inventory a bit, as he had a few slight explosions before he got his marvellous hair-styling machine to work.

But at last, after weeks of hard inventing, he shot out of his inventory, dragging the amazing device to show Mrs Flittersnoop.

It looked rather like an old-fashioned record-player.

"You turn this dial," said the Professor, "to select the kind of hair-style you want: fluffy, scraggy, bubbly, or straight. You can invent new looks by combining different styles."

"Well I never, I'm sure, sir," said Mrs Flittersnoop. "I was wondering what to do with this awful hair-style."

"Wonder no more!" cried the Professor. "Now you can have a new hair-style every day!"

Mrs Flittersnoop thought having a new hair-style every day was a bit much—it would be like having two baths a night—but she happily agreed to the Professor giving her a new one now,

since her present one was not only
frightful, but was getting a bit frayed
at the edges.

The Professor sat Mrs Flittersnoop
on the kitchen stool and stood the
machine beside her.

"What kind of, um, er, hair-style
would madam like?" he asked,
putting on a hairdressing voice.

Mrs Flittersnoop couldn't make up
her mind, so the Professor twiddled the
dial, pressed levers and hoped for the best.

Soon the room was full of a high-
class, beauty-parlour pong. Coloured
steam rose slowly from the machine, and
it made a noise like a second-hand
coffee-grinder.

"It tickles a bit,"
giggled Mrs Flittersnoop,
wriggling ever so slightly.

The professor pressed a lever and
turned a wheel. The machine stopped,
and Mrs Flittersnoop looked at herself
cautiously in the mirror.

"Well I never, indeed, I'm sure, sir,"
she said. "It's ever so much better than
the one Mr Percy Pompadour did, and
not so expensive!"

Next day Mr Percy Pompadour and all his girls arrived at the Professor's in a very hairdressing dither.

"I've just heard about your hair-styling machine, Professor," he squeaked. "You must get rid of it at once. It will ruin my business. People will come to you instead of me. I shall have to throw my girls out into the street."

Professor Branestawm couldn't quite see skinny little Mr Percy Pompadour throwing his girls into the street, since they were mostly on the large side and one of them looked as if she spent her holidays training on military assault courses.

"Nonsense," said the Professor. "You can put a lot of my machines into your salon and the girls will be able to attend to more customers in less, ah, um, time and so go home early, while you make more money by dealing with more customers."

So the machine was taken to Mr Percy Pompadour's salon, and in walked its first customer, Mrs Trumpington Smawl.

"I shall hold you responsible for any damage done to my hair, Professor," said Mrs Trumpington Smawl in her chilliest North Pole voice. "I don't expect that your machine will be able to do the Brush Back French Pleat Style I want, so it had better do something easier."

"Um," said the Professor, expecting trouble.

Clank, pop, bang, went the machine, getting ready to supply it. Coloured steam came out of the machine and the beauty-parlour pong erupted twice as smelly as before.

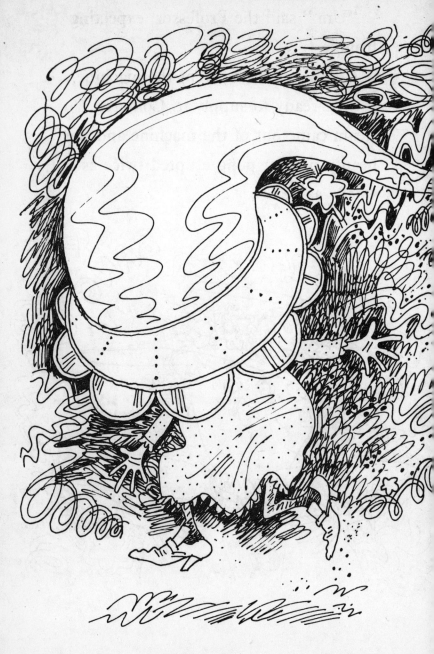

The machine set about Mrs Trumpington Smawl's hair to show her that no Branestawm invention was going to be defeated by a difficult hair-style. It gave her a Graduated Bob mixed up with a Layered Half-Cut with touches of an Edwardian Finger Wave.

"Stop it at once!" cried Mrs Trumpington Smawl.

The machine took no notice.

It gave her a cottage loaf hair-style on one side with a bun at the back, and went on to create a few jam tart, Swiss roll and apple pie styles of its own.

Mrs Trumpington Smawl wrenched herself free of the machine and rushed out of the salon and down the road, shrieking for her solicitor.

After her went the machine, pausing
only to put waves in the lamp-posts and
give hedges and bushes Bubble Cuts
and Edwardian Crops.

After them both rushed the Professor, waving his spectacles, and Mrs Flittersnoop, holding her new hair-style on with one hand and waving a wooden spoon with the other.

Shriek! Yell! Good gracious! Help!

The machine put frizzes
in an old man's hair,
beard and walking-stick ..

curls in a
stray cat's coat ...

and a window cleaner's
ladder was given
very special treatment.

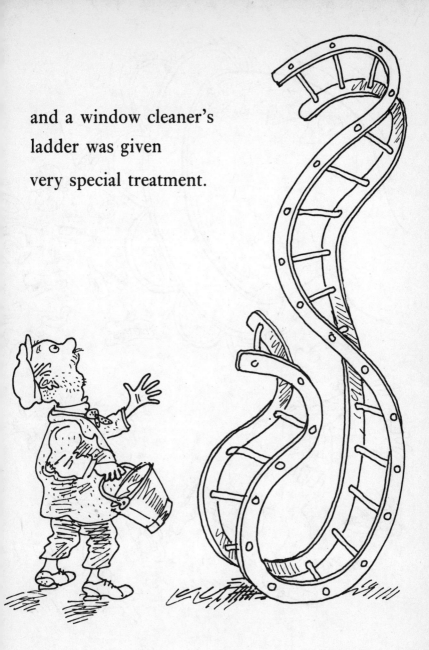

Then it caught sight of Bert's
Hot Dog van and went berserk.

Crash! Bang! Clank! Pop! Havoc reigned. The machine sucked Bert up, along with a whole heap of sausages, rolls, onions and a bottle of brown sauce . . .

The noise was alarming as the machine spat out curly sausages, permed onions and frizzy rolls.

Then, just as everyone was getting
very worried, the machine gave an
enormous sneeze ... and out shot Bert,
holding a pepper pot.

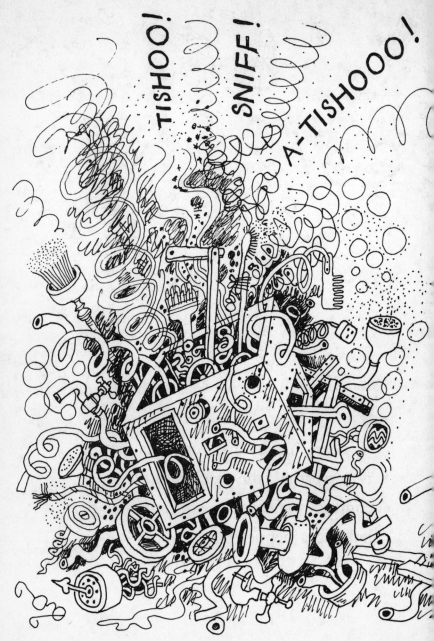

A-tishoo! A-tishoo! A-tishoo!
the machine couldn't stop sneezing ...
and at last—thank goodness—sneezed
itself to bits.

Mrs Flittersnoop packed the bits up
tidily into a box and sent them to the
local junk shop.

"Well, indeed, I'm sure, sir," gasped
Mrs Flittersnoop, when they got home.
"Thank goodness that's the last we shall
see of that *dreadful* machine!"

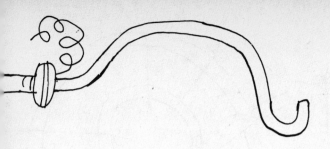

But it wasn't.

Colonel Dedshott, passing by the junk shop, saw the bits of machine and, not knowing what they were, bought them for the Professor.

"Thought they looked just the thing for you to make inventions with, what!" he said, curling up his moustache, as he presented them to the Professor the next day.

He set off to report to General Shatterfortz that all his soldiers were present and correct, while Mrs Flittersnoop gasped, "Oh no, indeed, I'm not sure at all, sir." But the Professor had already had . . .

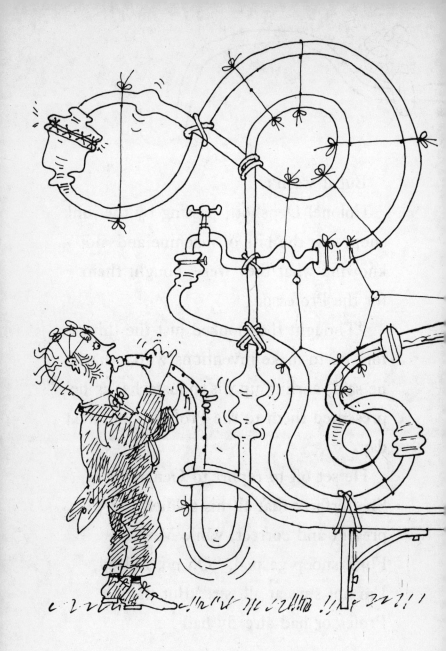

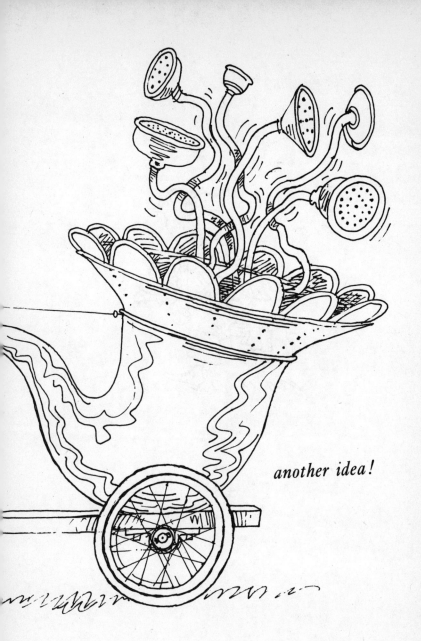

another idea!

Also in Young Puffin

ADVENTURE ON SKULL ISLAND

Tony Bradman

Life for a pirate family is one long adventure!

When Jim finds a treasure map of Skull Island on board the *Saucy Sally*, he knows he and his sister Molly are in for an exciting time. But little do they know that their great enemy, Captain Swagg, is after the same treasure – and is determined to get there first!

Also in Young Puffin

Willie Whiskers

Margaret Gordon

"I'm a hero," said Willie Whiskers. "I'm a hero because I eat too much and because I'm so fat."

Willie Whiskers is a very greedy little mouse – he is as round and fat as a hairy golf ball. But he doesn't care, even when he gets squashed in a slipper, tied up in a hair ribbon, or half drowned in a bowl of custard. His family think he should be doing sums instead, but all is forgiven the day Willie saves them from disaster, just because he *is* so fat!

Also in Young Puffin

Lion at School

Philippa Pearce

"I'm going to eat you up UNLESS you take me to school with you."

A growling lion spends a morning at school and frightens the school bully; a little boy saves a mouse's life; and the magic Great Sharp Scissors cause havoc!

THE LITTLE EXPLORER

Margaret Joy

Join Stanley on his thrilling voyage!

The little explorer is setting out on a long
journey. He is going in search of the
pinkafrillia, the rarest flower in the
world. Together with Knots, the sailor,
and Peckish, the parrot, Stanley travels
through the jungle of Allegria. And what
adventures they all have!